Athletics

Heather Rising

Contents

Athletics

What Is Athletics?

The sport of athletics, also called track and field, is a group of competitions testing human ability in running, jumping and throwing. Over time, competitions have developed to find the fastest and the strongest people.

There are athletics programs for all ages. Starting as young as three years old, athletes can become involved in fun activities, learn a new sport and compete against other athletes.

Today, the sport of athletics includes many different events that take place on and around a running track. Training for all athletics events keeps the body healthy and fit.

Young athletes participate in an athletics event by racing around a track.

These boys are competing in a cross-country running event, which takes place off the running track.

Ancient Sports

Ancient Egyptian art shows javelin throwing.

Athletics is one of the oldest sports in the world. Paintings of javelin-throwing competitions and marathon races have been found on the walls of 4000-year-old Egyptian tombs. In Ireland, there are books telling of the ancient Tailteann (pronounced *tell-shin*) Games. The games were thought to have been held since around 1820 **BCE**. They involved running and rock-throwing to honour the goddess Tailtiu (pronounced *tall-chu*).

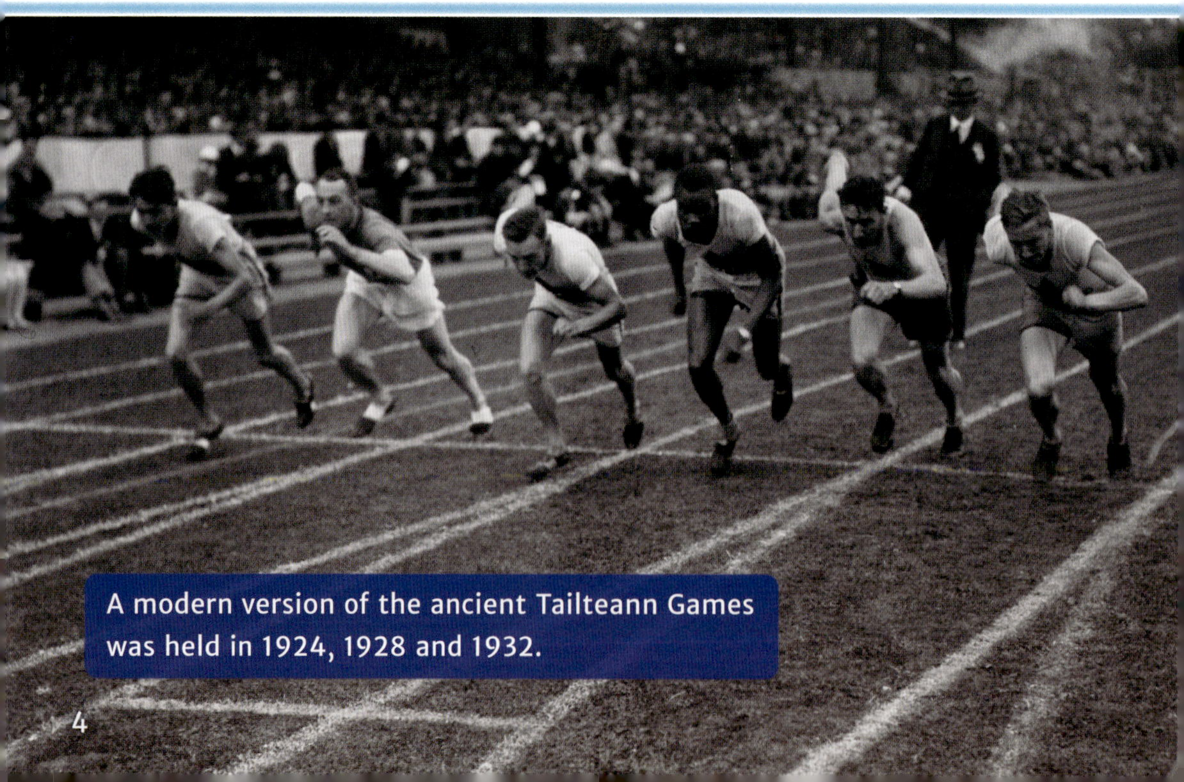

A modern version of the ancient Tailteann Games was held in 1924, 1928 and 1932.

The ancient Greeks invented athletics competitions as we know them now. They held an Olympic Games every four years, starting in 776 BCE. The first Olympic Games had only one competition, called the "stade", which was a 190-metre **sprint**. Later, more races were added. In some, the runner carried a **torch** or wore full armour. The ancient Greeks also added the long jump, the discus and the javelin throw to their five-day games.

The games were so popular, tens of thousands of visitors came to Olympia in southern Greece to watch them. The competitions even took place during times of war.

The word "athletics" comes from the Greek word *athlos*, meaning competition or contest.

The ancient Greeks held races where runners carried torches.

Modern Athletics Competitions

Athens, Greece, was the site of the first modern Olympic Games, held in 1896. Now, Olympic athletics competitions take place during the Summer Olympics, held every four years.

The first Olympic stadium was more narrow than the ones that are built today.

Modern stadiums are built to hold thousands of people.

Between Olympic Games, there are other athletics events and championship competitions. These give athletes the chance to train and compete with other athletes.

Modern athletics is a sport for all people and all ages. Athletes can participate in **professional** or non-professional competitions.

The World Athletics Championships, which began in 1976, are another chance for athletes to compete for medals. They take place every two years.

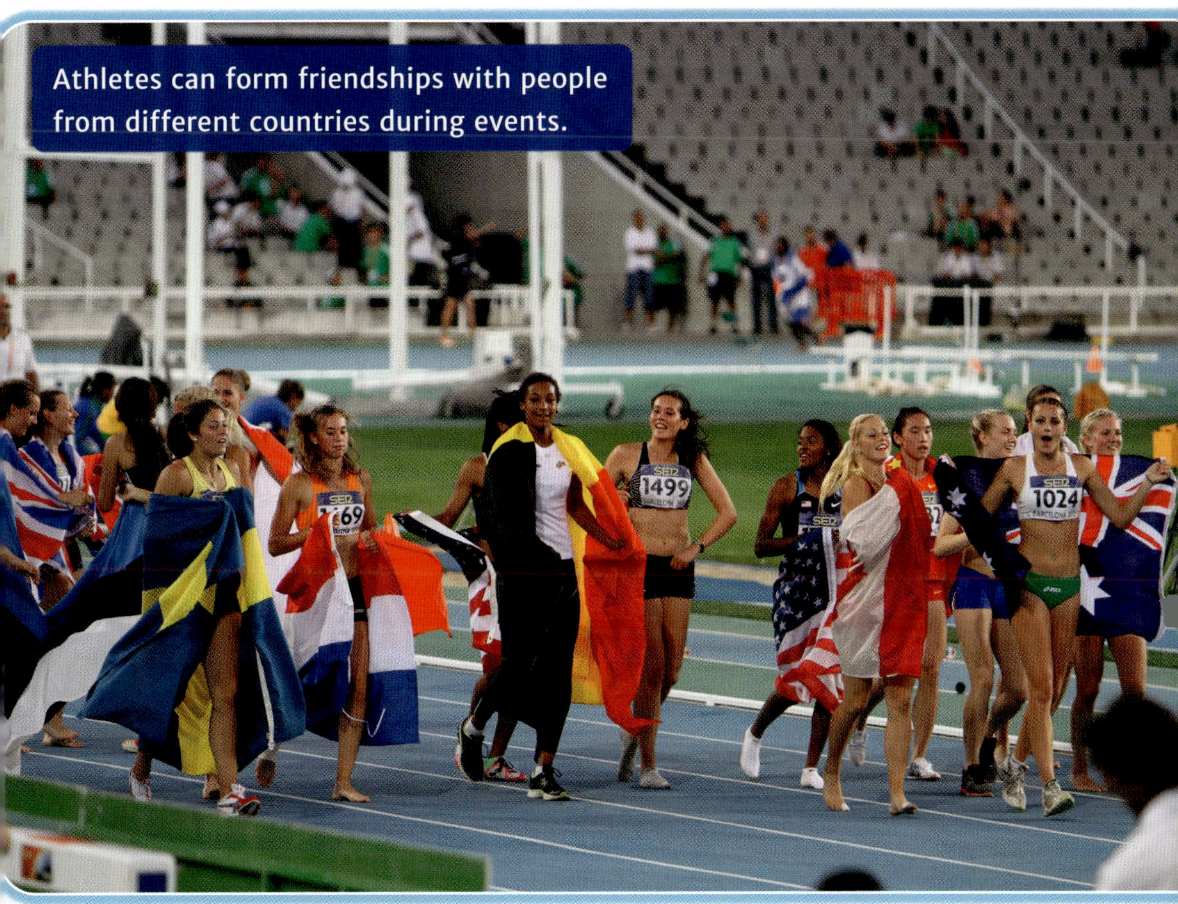

Athletes can form friendships with people from different countries during events.

The Track Sports

Athletics has many different types of running competitions. These mainly take place on a 400-metre oval-shaped track. There are several short sprint races, from 100 to 400 metres long, while the longest track race is 10 000 metres, or 25 laps around the track.

There are also short running and jumping races called **hurdles**.

Relay races take place on the track. In a relay race, a team of four runners take turns running part of the race, and they must pass a short stick called a "baton" to the next runner before they can start their turn.

Athletes learn a special way to jump over hurdles quickly.

Runners need to pass the baton carefully during a relay race.

There are other races that are held off the track. In cross-country running, athletes run different distances over grass, up hills or through forests. A marathon race is just over 42 kilometres and takes place on a road course. Race walking, a speed-walking race, can be as long as 20 kilometres or as short as 3000 metres (3 kilometres). The steeplechase is a 3000-metre race where athletes jump over 28 raised hurdles and 7 water hurdles.

Marathon races are held all over the world, like this one held in Serbia in 2016.

The Field Sports

The field events in athletics take place on the space inside the oval track. There are four jumping contests. High jumpers begin with a short run-up before leaping to clear a horizontal bar as high as two metres off the ground. Jumpers then land on a mat on the opposite side of the bar. The bar is raised after each successful jump. The jumper who clears the highest bar wins.

The pole vault also starts with a short sprint, but jumpers use a long pole to **propel** themselves over a horizontal bar. Jumpers can set their own bar height, but the win goes to the jumper who clears the highest bar.

The long jump begins with a run, then a jump, and ends with a landing in a sandpit.

The triple jump begins with a run, followed by a hop and a skip before the jumper lands in a sandpit. For both the long jump and the triple jump, the farthest measurement in the sandpit wins.

A pole vaulter uses a long pole to help her jump over a high bar.

Four different throwing events are common in athletics. In shot-put, a metal ball is thrown as far as possible from a marked circle.

The hammer throw involves athletes throwing a ball attached to a metal wire. The thrower stands in a marked circle and swings the ball before throwing. The longest throw wins.

In the discus event, an athlete first spins around in a marked circle before releasing a metal disc, called a discus. The discus can be as heavy as a two-litre bottle of water!

A javelin is a pole that is longer than two metres with a metal tip at one end. Athletes must throw it from above their shoulder, and it must land tip-first in the ground. The farthest throw wins.

Champion discus thrower Robert Harting from Germany spins before making his throw.

Para-athletics

Athletics is open to all athletes for training and competition. A para-athlete is an athlete who has a disability that affects their movements, senses or mental focus.

The first time that athletics was offered for para-athletes was in 1952, when a javelin-throwing contest was held for men who had been injured in World War II.

At the first Paralympic Games, held in Rome in 1960, there were 25 different medal events. By 1976, the Paralympic Games had grown to include events for athletes with **visual impairments**, such as blindness, and for **amputees**.

Athletes use special racing wheelchairs to compete in track events.

To keep competitions fair, para-athletes are grouped based on their ability to compete in their sport and the things they need to help them. A running guide, someone who runs beside the athlete, can help an athlete with a visual impairment to compete. A device such as a wheelchair or a **prosthetic** limb can also assist an athlete in their sport.

There are now more than 160 medal competitions in the Paralympic Games.

Athletes with prosthetic legs race against each other in the 2010 Paralympic World Cup.

Track Stars

Cathy Freeman is famous for being the first Australian First Nations athlete to win an individual Olympic gold medal. In the 2000 Sydney Olympics, Cathy Freeman memorably pulled ahead in the last 100 metres of the 400-metre sprint. She won the race with a time of 49.11 seconds.

Cathy Freeman pulls ahead in the 400-metre sprint at the 2000 Sydney Olympics.

Franz Nietlispach helped to develop a lighter wheelchair for para-athletes to use.

Franz Nietlispach celebrates his race finish at the 2000 Sydney Paralympics.

Franz Nietlispach (pronounced *neet-less-patch*), a Swiss para-athlete, has competed in every Paralympic Games from 1976 to 2008. He races different distances, from 400 to 10 000 metres. In total, he has won 14 gold, 7 silver and 2 bronze Paralympic medals for track events. He has also won the wheelchair category of the Boston Marathon in the USA five times.

Usain Bolt is a Jamaican athlete who is thought to be the fastest man alive. He broke his own 100-metre sprint world record at the 2009 World Championships in Berlin with a time of 9.58 seconds. He is the only person to win three **consecutive** Olympic gold medals in both the 100- and 200-metre sprints (in 2008, 2012 and 2016).

Usain Bolt winning the 100-metre sprint at the 2008 Beijing Olympics

World records can be set at any official competition, while Olympic records can only be set at the Olympic Games. Often, two different athletes can hold the world and the Olympic record for a sport.

Karsten Warholm celebrates after breaking the world record in the 400-metre hurdles at the Tokyo Olympics.

Norwegian athlete Karsten Warholm broke the 29-year-old record in the 400-metre hurdles by 0.08 seconds at a race in July 2021. Later that month, at the Tokyo Olympics, he broke his own record with a time of 45.94 seconds to win gold.

Competition Records

World records in athletics competitions continue to be broken, while some records remain in place for decades.

Bob Beamon, a US athlete, set a new Olympic and world record in the long jump in 1968. His long jump at the Mexico City Olympics was 55 centimetres farther than the previous record, and measured 8.90 metres. **Officials** at the event had to find a longer measuring tape to record the distance. His world record was broken by only 5 centimetres at the 1991 World Championships by another US athlete, Mike Powell. However, Bob Beamon's Olympic record still stands, more than 50 years later.

Bob Beamon's famous Olympic long jump in 1968

US athlete Jackie Joyner-Kersee set, and still holds, the world record for the heptathlon, winning gold at the 1988 Seoul Olympics with 7291 points. She is the first heptathlete to ever break 7000 points. Her long jump record from 1994 still holds second place in the world at 7.49 metres. She has won medals in four Olympics, winning the heptathlon gold again in 1992 at the Barcelona Olympics.

The heptathlon is a two-day competition with seven events. The order of events is: 100-metre hurdles, high jump, shot-put, 200-metre sprint, long jump, javelin and 800-metre run.

Jackie Joyner-Kersee competing in the 100-metre hurdles during the heptathlon at the 1988 Seoul Olympics

Jonathan Edwards, a British athlete, holds the record for the longest triple jump. He set an 18.29-metre record at the 1995 World Championships, and it remains unbroken. He won gold with a 17.71-metre triple jump at the 2000 Sydney Olympics.

Jonathan Edwards in the run-up to a triple jump at the 2000 Sydney Olympics

Zhang Liangmin, a para-athlete with a visual impairment, receives a gold medal at the 2016 Paralympic Games.

In the 2016 Paralympic Games in Rio de Janeiro, Zhang Liangmin from China beat the silver medallist's throw by 1.5 metres to win gold in the discus event, with a distance of 36.65 metres.
At the Tokyo Paralympics, held in 2021, Zhang Liangmin broke both her own and the world record, throwing 40.83 metres to win a third Paralympic gold medal.

Famous Moments in Athletics

There have been many memorable moments throughout the history of athletics competitions. Jesse Owens, an African American athlete, competed in the 1936 Berlin Olympics. He won four gold medals for sprints, relay and long jump. In many countries at that time, some people held **racist** beliefs about people of colour. When at home in the USA, Jesse Owens was not even able to stay in the same hotels as white athletes. Winning so many medals at the Olympics made Jesse Owens a symbol to show that all people should be treated equally.

Jesse Owens competing in the 200-metre sprint during the 1936 Berlin Olympics

Mo Farah (second from left, on the outside) catching up during the 10 000-metre race after falling

Mo Farah is a British long-distance runner who has set records and won medals throughout his career. He has won Olympic gold medals in both the 5000- and 10 000-metre races. During the 2016 Rio de Janeiro Olympics, he tripped on the tenth lap of the 10 000-metre race. After falling, he got back up, overtook the lead runner and won the gold medal in 27 minutes and 5.17 seconds. He crossed the finish line just 0.47 seconds ahead of the silver medal winner.

Mo Farah celebrates his wins by creating an "M" with his arms.

Olympic Spirit

Professional athletics is highly competitive, since athletes are trying to be the best in the world, but it can also reveal wonderful moments of fairness and friendship.

During the 1936 Berlin Olympics, two Japanese friends, Shuhei Nishida and Sueo Oe, were competing in the pole vault. Towards the end of the event, the two athletes were tied in second place. Knowing a jump-off would mean one would take bronze and the other silver, they refused to jump again. They asked officials if they could share the silver, but they were turned down. Using their earlier jumps, it was decided that Shuhei Nishida should win silver and Sueo Oe the bronze. When the pair returned home, they had their medals turned into two half-silver and half-bronze medals. These became known as the "Medals of Friendship".

Shuhei Nishida (left) and Sueo Oe (right) receiving their medals at the 1936 Berlin Olympics

In 2021, close friends Gianmarco Tamberi of Italy and Mutaz Essa Barshim of Qatar were tied for the gold medal in high jump at the Tokyo Olympics. The two athletes were asked if they would like to have a jump-off to decide the winner. They said they would like to share the gold instead. The official agreed, and they both won a gold medal.

Gianmarco Tamberi (left) and Mutaz Essa Barshim (right) with their shared gold medals at the Tokyo Olympics

New Zealand runner Nikki Hamblin crashed and fell in the 5000-metre race during the 2016 Rio de Janeiro Olympics. An American, Abbey D'Agostino, fell over her. Once D'Agostino got to her feet, she reached down and helped Hamblin up. They both began to run, but D'Agostino was injured and collapsed. This time, Hamblin offered D'Agostino help, and both were able to finish the race.

Nikki Hamblin stopped to help Abbey D'Agostino in their 5000-metre race at the 2016 Rio de Janeiro Olympics.

At the Tokyo Olympics held in 2021, Isaiah Jewett from the USA and Nijel Amos from Botswana fell in the 800-metre race. The two helped each other up and crossed the finish line together with their arms around each other.

Isaiah Jewett and Nijel Amos decided to finish the 800-metre race together at the Tokyo Olympics.

The wide variety of events in athletics encourages athletes to find their own strengths. While competing to break records and win medals, athletes develop the courage to be their very best. As they travel around the world to compete, athletes share an excitement for their sport and form new friendships.

How to Do the Long Jump

Goal

To do a long jump

Materials

• a pair of good running shoes

• a sandpit to land in

• a launch pad

• a 30-metre runway

• a measuring tape

Steps

1. Warm up your muscles by stretching both your arms and legs.
2. Find your "take-off" foot. This is the foot that you will use to launch from the pad. You might need to try a few jumps to find which is your best foot to jump with.

3. Decide how far you will need to run before the jump. Walk that distance back from the launch pad in front of the sandpit. The best distance is different for each jumper.
4. Starting with your take-off foot, sprint down the runway. Increase your speed as you go. Keep looking straight ahead, and focus on a landing point in the sandpit.

5. As you reach the pit, plant your take-off foot flat on the pad. Then, use that foot to push yourself off the ground. You can jump from any point before or on the pad. If your foot crosses the end of the launch pad, the jump is a called a **foul**.

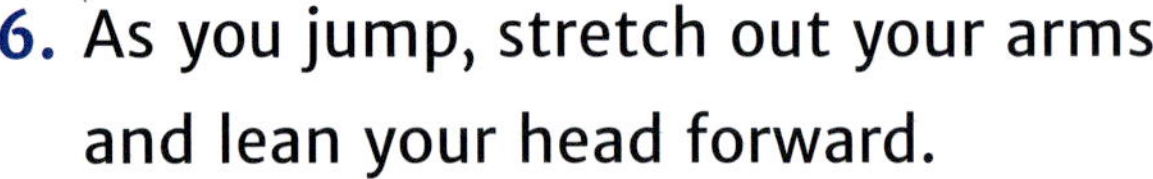

6. As you jump, stretch out your arms and lean your head forward.

7. Try to fall forward, so that you don't place your hands behind you as you land in the sandpit, since your distance will be measured from the closest mark.

8. Find the distance of your jump with a measuring tape. Measure from the end of the pad to the closest mark in the sand.

You have three tries.

The competitor with the longest fair jump is the winner!

Glossary

amputees (*noun*) people who have lost an arm or a leg after an accident or an illness

BCE (*adjective*) Before the Common Era, the time dates are counted from

consecutive (*adjective*) following one after the other

foul (*noun*) a move that breaks a rule in a competition

hurdles (*noun*) a race where athletes jump over obstacles

officials (*noun*) people whose job is to make decisions at events such as competitions

professional (*adjective*) done as a job, rather than a hobby

propel (*verb*) to cause something to move forwards or upwards

prosthetic (*adjective*) human-made as a replacement for a part of the body, such as an arm or a leg

racist (*adjective*) unfair towards people because of their race or the colour of their skin

sprint (*noun*) a run at full speed over a short distance

torch (*noun*) a small stick with a burning top

visual impairments (*noun*) part or full blindness in one or both eyes

Index